SICK DAY JITTERS

JULIE DANNEBERG
ILLUSTRATED BY JUDY LOVE

Charlesbridge

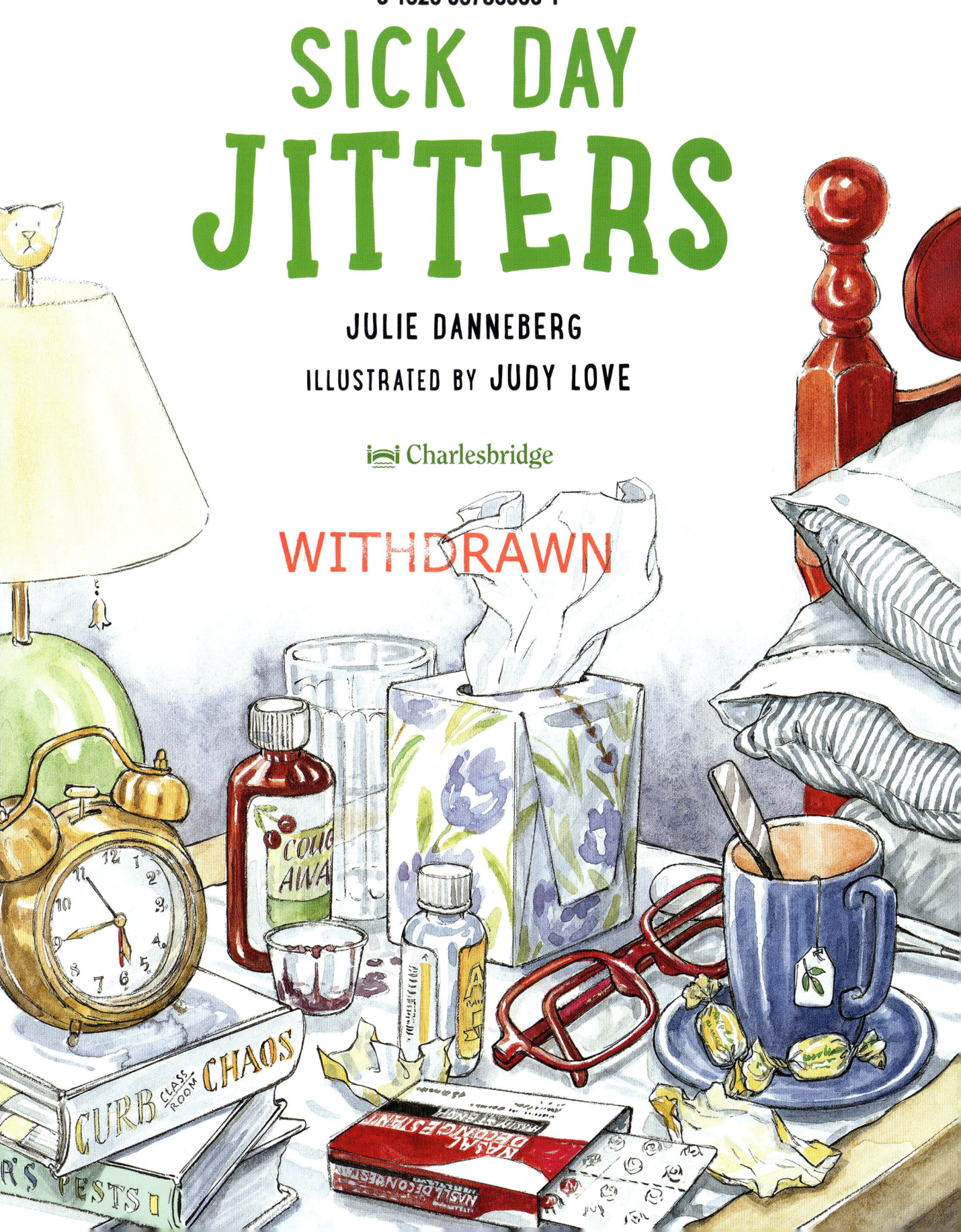

For Emmy, Zoey, and Kennedy. I love you!—J. D.

For my dear friend, Sue, with love.—J. L.

Text copyright © 2023 by Julie Danneberg
Illustrations copyright © 2023 by Judy Love
All rights reserved, including the right of reproduction in whole or in part in any form.
Charlesbridge and colophon are registered trademarks of Charlesbridge Publishing, Inc.

At the time of publication, all URLs printed in this book were accurate and active. Charlesbridge, the author, and the illustrator are not responsible for the content or accessibility of any website.

Published by Charlesbridge
9 Galen Street
Watertown, MA 02472
(617) 926-0329
www.charlesbridge.com

Library of Congress Cataloging-in-Publication Data
Names: Danneberg, Julie, 1958– author. | Love, Judy, 1953– illustrator.
Title: Sick day jitters / Julie Danneberg; illustrated by Judy Love.
Description: Watertown, MA: Charlesbridge, [2023] | Audience: Ages 5–8. | Audience: Grades 2–3. | Summary: "When Mrs. Hartwell is out sick and her substitute doesn't show up, the teachers and staff at the school pitch in to help."—Provided by publisher.
Identifiers: LCCN 2022031568 (print) | LCCN 2022031569 (ebook) | ISBN 9781623544249 (hardcover) | ISBN 9781623544256 (paperback) | ISBN 9781632893857 (ebook)
Subjects: LCSH: Elementary school teachers—Juvenile fiction. | Sick—Juvenile fiction. | School children—Juvenile fiction. | Electronic mail messages—Juvenile fiction. | Humorous stories. | CYAC: Teachers—Fiction. | Sick—Fiction. | School children—Fiction. | Electronic mail messages—Fiction. | Humorous stories. | LCGFT: Humorous fiction.
Classification: LCC PZ7.D2327 Si 2023 (print) | LCC PZ7.D2327 (ebook) | DDC [E]—dc23
LC record available at https://lccn.loc.gov/2022031568
LC ebook record available at https://lccn.loc.gov/2022031569

Printed in China
(hc) 10 9 8 7 6 5 4 3 2 1
(pb) 10 9 8 7 6 5 4 3 2 1

Illustrations done in watercolor, transparent dyes, and India ink on Strathmore paper
Display type set in Lunchbox by Kimmy Designs
Text type set in Electra by Adobe Systems Incorporated
Art digitizing and printing by 1010 Printing International Limited in Huizhou, Guangdong, China
Production supervision by Mira Kennedy
Designed by Diane M. Earley

Mrs. Hartwell woke up sick. Very sick. Stuffy-nose, scratchy-throat, achy-bones sick. Too-sick-to-go-to-work sick. She called in to request a substitute teacher and then went right back to sleep.